# Mama Went Walking

By Christine Berry • Illustrated by María Cristina Brusca

Henry Holt and Company • New York

Published by Henry Holt and Company, Inc.,
115 West 18th Street, New York, New York 10011.
Published in Canada by Fitzhenry & Whiteside Limited,
195 Allstate Parkway, Markham, Ontario L3R 4T8.

Library of Congress Cataloging-in-Publication Data
Berry, Christine.
    Mama went walking / by Christine Berry ; illustrated by María
Cristina Brusca.
    Summary: Sarah saves her mother from a series of imaginary
dangers, from lions in the Jaba-Jaba Jungle to scritchy-witchy
things in the Gonagetcha Forest.
    ISBN 0-8050-1261-3
    [1. Mothers and daughters—Fiction.   2. Imagination—Fiction.]
I. Brusca, María Cristina, ill.   II. Title.
PZ7.B46165Mam   1990
[E]—dc20          89-39789

Henry Holt books are available at special discounts
for bulk purchases for sales promotions, premiums,
fund-raising, or educational use. Special editions
or book excerpts can also be created to specification.

For details contact:

Special Sales Director
Henry Holt and Company, Inc.
115 West 18th Street
New York, New York 10011

First Edition .
Designed by Maryann Leffingwell
Printed in the United States of America
10 9 8 7 6 5 4 3 2 1

*For my own "Mama," Ann Waller, with love    —C.B.*

*To Ana Jimena Martínez and her Mama    —M.C.B.*

Mama says she loves me. Mama says she needs me. When Mama goes adventuring, I'm never far behind.

Mama went exploring in the Jaba-Jaba Jungle.

There were lions in the trees. There were lions in the weeds. There were prowling, growling lions all around.

"I think these lions are hungry," said Mama.

I fed them hamburgers and they went away.

"Thank you, Sarah," said Mama.
"You're welcome," I replied.

Mama went riding in the Ropacactus Canyon.

There were storms above the mountains. There was lightning in the sky. There was roiling, boiling water coming down.

"I can't outride this flash flood," said Mama.
I lassoed Mama, horse and all, from my helicopter.
"Thank you, Sarah," said Mama.
"Anytime," I replied.

Mama went canoeing down the Rattlesnake River.

There were rattlers on the rocks. There were rattlers in the water. There were rude and raucous rattlers all around.

"I wish these snakes would quiet down," said Mama.
I played a lullaby on my harmonica and all those rattlers went
to sleep.
"Thank you, Sarah," said Mama.
"No problem," I replied.

Mama went climbing on the Dinosaur Rocks.

There were cracks and faulty footholds. There were cliffs and there were crags. There were brontosaurus boulders crashing down.

"I think I'm going to fall," said Mama.

I threw her my umbrella and she floated to the ground.
"Thank you, Sarah," said Mama.
"My pleasure," I replied.

Mama went sailing on the Jellyfish Sea.

There were waves as big as giants. There were whales and there were sharks. There was black and salty water all around.

"I think I'm sinking," said Mama.

I was swimming with the dolphins so I towed her boat to shore.

"Thank you, Sarah," said Mama.
"Anything for you," I replied.

Mama went spelunking in the Blackenbatty Caves.

Bears were sleeping. Bears were snoozing. Bears were barely dreaming dreams. There were roaring, snoring grizzlies all around.

"It's much too noisy in here," said Mama.
I turned those bears over on their sides and they stopped
snoring.
"Thank you, Sarah," said Mama.
"It was nothing," I replied.

Mama went walking in the Gonagetcha Forest.

It was dark and getting darker. There were eyes behind the trees. There were scritchy, witchy noises all around.

Gonagetcha Forest! Dark and getting darker! *What* behind the trees?

Eyes!
"And scritchy, witchy noises all around," said Mama.

"This place is too scary for me," I said.
Mama hugged me and the forest disappeared.

"Thank you, Mama," I said.
"Anytime," Mama replied.

"I love you, Mama."
"I love you, too, Sarah."

Mama says she loves me. Mama says she needs me.
When Mama goes adventuring, I'm never far behind.